LOVE STARS

RED THREAD THEORY

RUDRA

INDIA · SINGAPORE · MALAYSIA

ISBN

Harecase 979-8-89133-985-9
Paperback 979-8-89133-926-2

Contents

15th August 2011

In the ever-famous words of some old guy, "America, the Land of Opportunity." That's what they say, right? When my feet first hit American soil, I swear I could hear the crackle of dreams sizzling in the air, like the first sweet drop of pancake batter on a hot griddle. I, Rudra - yes, that's me, PhD hopeful and a guy with stars in his eyes – was ready to leap into the intellectual maelstrom and wrestle with books till the break of dawn.

Fast-forward to the slow, screeching burn that peeled the star-spangled varnish off my dreams. There's this thing about being foreign - you're like a rare trading card, exotic until someone decides you're not in the deck they want to play. I went from being Rudra, the guy with questions bigger than the universe, to being "that guy" – you know, the one who's "different". And it's like, this whole place suddenly turned into this messed-up labyrinth. I swear I could hear minotaurs snarling behind every hallowed hall.

Then came the storm, a dark and messy one, where my work, my words, my everything was stomped on by the very boots I thought were marching alongside me.

When I felt all was lost, I turned to the justice system. Yeah, it gave me a high-five with the back of its hand.

Let me take you on a journey through my very own Portrait of the Student as a Young Man in Despair. Imagine, Rudra, with eyes that used to sparkle like the midnight sky, entering the sacred realm of academia. Picture the nine Olympians of the college, the professors who are almost mythic, choosing me, yes me, to bask in the brilliance of their wisdom.

As the days turned into weeks, and the weeks into months, the walls of this institution that I thought were built with dreams and possibilities began to close in on me. The air became heavy, thick with a bitterness that seemed to seep out of the very bricks. I, who prided myself in questioning and seeking truths, found that my contrarian views were being branded as sacrilege. The taste of failing grades was a bitter pill, hard to swallow.

It was like being caught in a maze with no exit in sight. My mind was whirring, my soul was in turmoil, and I was gasping for air. I reached out to one of the nine titans, Sri, a fellow countryman. Surely, he, who had walked a mile in my shoes, would provide me with guidance and solace.

Sri's words were gentle as a whisper, suggesting that perhaps it was all just a terrible mistake. He advised me to report the incident and to seek justice.

Oh, what dreams of justice and vindication danced in my head! The committee was called together - it was as if a council of sages had been assembled to decide the fate of a nation. And among them was Sri! My heart leapt; I was not alone. I had my stalwart ally, or so I thought.

But, as the proceedings commenced, my hopes began to crumble. The Sri I thought would be my guardian turned out to be a mere shadow of a man. His silence echoed through the room. He was there in body, but his spirit was absent. He was just a spectre, nodding along with every word that sought to crush my spirit.

And then it happened. The tempest of emotions I'd been keeping at bay swept through me like a raging storm. Anger, frustration, sorrow, despair - a maelstrom of every emotion known to man ripped through the core of my being. I felt like a mariner lost at sea, with no guiding star to lead me to safe shores.

The hallowed halls that were meant to be a sanctuary for my dreams became an icy labyrinth. The cold was bone-deep, the maze, never-ending. The minotaur that had been snarling in the shadows lunged with full force, and I was left unarmed, with no thread to lead me out of the dark.

There, in that committee room, I felt smaller than an atom in the vast universe. My voice, which had always been my weapon, my strength, was reduced to a whisper, lost in the cacophony of judgment and rejection. There was a moment, just a split second, where the weight of the world was so heavy that I thought I would simply disappear.

But then something happened.

As I stumbled out of the room, the last vestiges of hope dissipating like the morning mist, I felt something inside me. It was faint at first, like the whisper of wind through leaves, but then it grew, pulsating through my veins like wildfire.

There was something else I hadn't lost. Something that the halls of this academic labyrinth couldn't touch.

I remembered this joke of a thing that my "friend"(let's call her that for now) keeps telling: the Red Thread. Not the kind your grandma sews buttons with. No, this thread was way cooler. The ancient kind that's supposed to be tied to your soul and stretches across space and time to the soul of your One True... something.

That's when the floodgates opened and the memory of this "friend" burst through. Oh, Aisha. Her eyes were galaxies, and her laugh was like a hundred pop rocks all doing their ecstatic dance in your mouth at once. We were like, partners in crime - stealing mangoes and planning world domination under the ancient banyan tree. I never realized that my heart had this VIP section roped off, and it was Aisha who was on the guest list.

My go-to reaction to this whole Red Thread shindig had been pretty much set in stone until, well, this very nanosecond. I would cheerfully crown her "Lady Loony of the Lunar Threads" because, let's be real, banking on some age-old myth that's probably the brainchild of moon fairies with too much time on their hands, seemed Loony to me.

There I was, marooned in my room that had all the ambience of a cardboard box left out in the rain, when I felt this tingle like my soul got a text message, I felt this electric pull. I wasn't sure if it was a cosmic SMS or my heart hitting redial over and over and trying to find comfort in her thoughts, but it felt like something was tugging me, something unbreakable, unshakeable, a line that connected me and Aisha.

Do I find myself inclining toward belief in the Red Thread now? I don't think so, or so my sceptical heart chooses to believe. But one thing I know for sure is my thoughts were filled with Aisha.

With a heavy heart, I made the decision. I was going to return to India. It wasn't what I had planned, and every fibre in my body resisted the notion. But somehow, it felt like the winds were pushing my sails in that direction. My soul ached for something genuine, something that would heal the scars and revive the embers of hope within me. Maybe it was the Red Thread, maybe it was just desperation for change, or maybe it was a bit of both. Either way, I needed to see if the land I called home could stitch my fragmented spirit back together. My heart had been longing for something, and maybe, just maybe, it was hidden in the embrace of my roots, where laughter danced in the monsoons and the ancient banyan trees whispered secrets of belonging.

My story wasn't ending here. No way. I am the Shah Rukh Khan of this story, complete with dimples and charm, I end up with this girl, and come on top of this storm before the credits roll.

20th June 2011

As the plane cuts through the sky, streaking towards the land of monsoons and mangos, my mind is a torrent. The air inside the cabin feels thin as if it's in short supply, just like the courage in my heart. But something else is stirring – memories, moments long past but never forgotten. And through the tempest, there is Aisha.

Aisha... the wind carries her name like a chant through time. She was older than me, but it's not like I kept a mental score. It's just that life had this annoying habit of chalking up numbers next to everything – years, grades, timelines. But when it came to Aisha, numbers were puny warriors who just couldn't storm the citadel of my heart.

The 'how' of our first meeting? Well, the memory mist swallows that one whole. Our families had been painting the same social canvas for aeons, and as toddlers, we were inevitably splattered in that same picture. One of the precious droplets in my ocean of memories, though, is of us vacationing in her family's home in Wellington, in the Nilgiris. Heaven, my friend, had a postal address back then, and it was there.

The place was a page out of a fairy tale – the clouds weaving dreams through the trees, the dew-kissed leaves whispering secrets, and us – two wildlings on the cusp of innocence, living as if the world was painted only in hues of freedom.

I didn't know what this warm, fuzzy feeling was when I was around Aisha. I mean, come on, the only butterflies I knew were the ones with wings!

However, that very night... left a permanent mark etched in the depths of my soul.

I was cosy in bed, likely dreaming of owning the coolest toy car, when I was jolted awake by a deafening sound - a cross between thunder and a cacophony of pots having an existential crisis. The pressure cooker in the kitchen had exploded with manic fury.

There we were, a battalion of half-asleep, confused souls, with eyes wider than the full moon. In that sea of faces, my eyes were on a treasure hunt. Aisha. Where was she? My heartbeats felt like they would tear through my chest. It was as if a thousand restless spirits were pounding on the walls, asking, screaming, yearning to know if she was safe.

But let's hit the pause button here. You see, the tendrils of the past have a peculiar way of entangling with the heartstrings of the present.

Here I am, several time zones and a lifetime away from that night, and the same symphony is playing. I'm panting, restless. The air is thick with the same desperation, and my eyes are searching, starving for a glimpse of Aisha.

I can't shake off the feeling that Aisha's around. Like, I need to see her, talk to her, laugh with her. Remember that Red Thread Aisha used to talk about? I kinda feel like there's something tugging at me.

The plane kisses the earth and I am jolted back into the now. My feet touch Indian soil and I feel a heady mix of déjà vu and nostalgia flooding my senses. The air is rich, laden with the scent of spices and the promises of monsoons. Is this home? The question lingers like a wisp of cloud in the morning sky.

My phone buzzes with a message from my mom: "Welcome back, Rudra! Your room is ready, just as you left it."

My room... a place where I dreamt, laughed, cried, grew. I'll revisit it soon. Right now, I long to see the old banyan trees, to feel the monsoon rain, to hear a familiar laugh - Aisha's laugh.

Aisha, are you still here?

That old story about the Red Thread doesn't seem so silly anymore. It feels like a trail in the woods, a signpost pointing me home.

So here I am, taking my first steps back into my past, hoping to find the threads that will stitch my life back together.

5th May 2012

Touching down in Bangalore, I find the city bustling with the same energy, the same pulse I left behind years ago. The familiar smell of petrichor meets my nostrils, the monsoon rains have just swept through, leaving the air fresher, purer. The skyline remains punctuated by the silhouette of familiar structures - the UB City, the Vidhana Soudha, and the numerous tech parks that dot the city reminding me that Bangalore is and always will be, a blend of tradition and modernity.

Driving through the wide streets towards my home, the city hums its welcome. The vibrant graffiti adorning the city walls catches my eye, a visual symphony of colors that were not there when I left. The city's spirit of creativity, and its dynamism hasn't waned, it has only grown, morphed into something more beautiful, more resilient.

The mango tree outside our house still stands tall, a silent witness to the tales of time. It's grown, much like the city, much like me. It stands firm, its gnarled bark embedded with countless tales of time. It has grown, much like Bangalore. Much like me. It's a silent, gentle reminder of the impermanence of everything and yet, the unwavering continuity of life. The tree and I, we share our stories - stories of growth, change, and resilience.

Beneath its broad leaves, I feel a certain kinship with it. Its roots have plunged deeper, as have mine. While it has borne the brunt of countless storms and sunny days, it remains unbowed, unbroken. I too have weathered my storms, have stood under the blazing sun of adversities, but here I am, unbowed, unbroken, perhaps even stronger.

My parents have aged; the signs are subtle yet noticeable. The lines on my father's face, etched deeper, his hair, a mix of black and grey. My mother moves slower, yet there's a grace in her steps, an elegance that time has bestowed upon her. Their smiles though, they're unchanged - warm, comforting, home.

It's been a week and I feel calmer, more in control. The sky is a clear blue and the sun casts its golden rays - a reminder of life's promise of growth, change and resilience.

The city's pulse thrums through me, a rhythm I had forgotten but now moves me with an irresistible beat. The music of honking vehicles, the chorus of vendors at the street corners, the symphony of life that unfolds every day on these familiar streets. They resonate within me, tuning out the distant hum of my past life.

The memories of the USA, of gleaming skyscrapers scraping the sky, of ceaseless days and nights spent in a dizzying professional race, are now slowly fading. They feel like echoes bouncing off from a canyon - distant, intangible, their essence losing ground to the vibrancy of my here and now.

I find myself succumbing to the warm embrace of familiarity that Bangalore wraps me in. Its energetic buzz, its vibrant hues, its mix of the traditional and the modern, they're all softly erasing the sharp edges of my past. The cacophony that I had once left behind is now a lullaby that sings me to peace.

The challenges, the memories - they all feel like a dream that is losing its vividness with each passing day. They're being replaced by the tang of filter coffee, the lilting tune of a Kannada song playing somewhere, the warm smiles of familiar faces, and the comforting touch of my childhood bed. The scar of the past seems to be gradually healing, replaced by the soothing balm of home. It's not just a return to a physical place, it's a journey back to myself.

My weeks turn into a whirlwind of reconnecting with old friends, those bonds, dusted by time but unbroken. There's Anitha, my junior. Her infectious laughter and quick wit remind me of the good old college days. We spend hours reminiscing, reliving the past, and discussing the future.

She offers me a sit-down with her boss.

The Boss appreciating the unique expertise and global exposure I bring says "You've always been brilliant. Your reputation precedes you, Rudra," he tells me, his words are not flattery but a reaffirmation of a truth I had almost forgotten. The offer isn't what makes my day; it's the recognition of my worth, the acknowledgement of my skills.

The job offer brings a welcome routine to my life, promising me National and Global exposure, working at the World's No.1 dental company was no ordinary feat. It's a place where I find purpose, a place where I can make a difference. The warmth of the grateful smiles of patients, make the nightmares of my past recede into the shadows.

Then there's Meera, who teaches at a local school and has a knack for baking the best chocolate cake. There's Ravi, the tech wizard, whose startup is now gaining national attention. Catching up with them feels like therapy.

Bangalore's symphony has become mine. Its rhythm pulsates in sync with my heart, and I sway to its tune. Each honk, every Kannada phrase, and the aroma of filter coffee contribute to the harmonious melody that is Bangalore — the essence of my existence.

But in all of this warmth, in all of this familiarity, there's a missing note - Aisha. I still haven't been able to find her, and the absence feels like a missing tooth, unnoticed by all but sorely felt by one.

I find myself looking for her in the old haunts, hoping to catch a glimpse of her smile, to hear her laughter. But she remains elusive. A part of me yearns for her, but I decide to let destiny play its hand. If we are meant to cross paths, we will.

Every passing face on the crowded streets, every ring of my phone, stirs a tidal wave of hope, only to recede into a painful realization of her continued absence. The bookstore where we'd spend hours debating over authors, the lake where we'd shared our dreams, now stand as quiet reminders of a past that I yearn to grasp but slips through like sand.

Amidst the swirling maelstrom of my emotions, a profound revelation begins to dawn. While I cherish the past, I am no longer the person I was. The past years have not just left their marks on the landscape of Bangalore but have chiseled and shaped my personality too. I've matured, grown, developed resilience, learned to face adversities head-on, and above all, understood the art of letting go.

I've realized that not all questions have immediate answers, not all wounds heal quickly, and not all missing chords can be found when you need them. Like the sacred river caressing the heart of India, life too has its pace, its rhythm, and its course.

It dawns on me that Aisha is not merely a person but a symbol of a past I've left behind, a past that I subconsciously yearn for amidst the realities of the present. She personifies a longing for a simpler time, a reminder of who I was and who I've become.

Time moves on.

The first day of work is a moment of reconciliation with my past and an affirmation of my future. The smell of antiseptic, the sound of the dental drill, and the smiles of relieved patients become a symphony of normalcy that slowly fills the silent voids of my life. The rhythm of my daily routine anchors me, its familiarity an antidote to the throbbing ache of Aisha's absence.

In the evenings, I often take to walking. The city's streets, bustling with vendors and filled with the aroma of street food, become a maze of discoveries. I begin to rediscover Bangalore, not just as a city but as an integral part of my identity. Every street corner, every graffiti, every smell and sound add a layer to my understanding of this city and of myself.

I visit Cubbon Park, its green expanse a contrast to the concrete jungle outside. The lush trees, the myriad hues of blooming flowers, and the sporadic chirping of birds create a soothing cocoon of serenity. Here, amidst the hushed whispers of nature, I reflect on the complexities of my journey.

The meandering pathways of the park become a metaphor for my life - twisting and turning, sometimes leading to beautiful vistas and at other times, towards unfamiliar terrain.

Yet, as I navigate my present, the ghost of my past lingers. Aisha's absence often emerges from the corners of my memories, a bittersweet reminder of what I have lost. Her laughter, her teasing words, the way her eyes lit up when she spoke about her dreams - they continue to haunt my solitude.

There are times when I fight the urge to seek her out, to find answers. But there's a part of me that recognizes the need for patience, for allowing life to unravel its mysteries at its own pace.

My days pass in this flux of emotions, oscillating between acceptance and longing, joy and sorrow, connection and solitude.

In these ordinary days, in the quiet moments of solitude, in the bursts of laughter with old friends, and in the familiar routine of work, I am gradually finding myself.

Aisha may remain an unfinished chapter of my past, but she no longer dictates my present or my future. She is a part of my memory, a part of my journey, but she is not my destination.

13th February 2014

The drive to Nandi Hills becomes a journey through time. Leaving behind the city's chaos, I traverse through villages that still retain the flavor of old-world India. Mud houses with thatched roofs, cows lazily chewing cud, children playing in open fields, women drawing water from wells - it's like walking through the pages of a R.K. Narayan novel.

The winding road up to Nandi Hills is dotted with viewpoints offering breathtaking vistas of the cityscape and the verdant landscape beyond. As the car winds its way up the serpentine road, I feel the city's cacophony fading, replaced by the whisper of the wind and the occasional chirping of birds.

Standing at the summit of Nandi Hills, I am met with a panoramic view that leaves me speechless. Below, the world spreads out in an infinite sprawl of green interspersed with patches of civilization. The vast sky overhead, the city's distant skyline, the verdant valley below - they converge to paint a picture of surreal beauty.

Despite the breathtaking view, my mind drifts back to the city, to the mango tree outside my house, to Aisha. It's strange how she still manages to occupy my thoughts despite my attempts to move on. Her memory is like the wind, unpredictable and pervasive, brushing past me when least expected.

As I watch the sun slowly descend, painting the sky with hues of red and orange, I can't help but think of how life is full of paradoxes. Just like the setting sun, the past, no matter how brightly it burns, must eventually give way to the night - the present.

And like the promise of a new dawn after a dark night, the future too waits with its own mysteries and possibilities. But as I stand there, I realize that I can only truly appreciate the sunrise if I accept the sunset. I must learn to let go of the past to make way for the present.

The journey back home is a quiet one, the silence punctuated only by the hum of the car's engine and the occasional hoot of an owl. The city lights gradually become visible, drawing me back into its vibrant chaos.

As I navigate the winding road back from Nandi Hills, the soft strains of a familiar melody playing from my car's stereo, my phone buzzes on the dashboard, disturbing the tranquility. I glance at the screen, assuming it to be a call from Aman or perhaps a patient, but what I see makes my heart stutter. "Aisha," the screen reads. A message from Aisha.

I stare at it, the tiny illuminated name on the screen somehow making the world around me blur into insignificance. My hands tighten around the steering wheel, my knuckles going white. It's a sudden plunge into icy water, a jolt of electricity. My mind stumbles, my breath catches. An unexpected shock, a moment of disbelief. I pull over to the side of the road, the purr of the car's engine in the quiet night providing a stark contrast to the storm of emotions brewing within me.

A thousand questions flood my mind. Why now? What could she possibly want to say after all these years? Is it an old message that got delayed? Or has she been thinking about me just as I have been thinking about her?

My finger hovers over the notification, but I pull it back, as if the message were a live wire. It's not the message that frightens me, it's the tsunami of emotions it threatens to unleash. For the longest time, I had hoped for this, prayed for a sign from her, a chance to reconnect. But now that it's here, right at my fingertips, I am seized by a strange sense of fear and confusion.

I've been steadily rebuilding my life, brick by brick, finding solace in the familiar and the mundane. I've been healing, or at least I thought I was.

My heart longs to open the message, to take what feels like the first real breath in years. But my mind, always the more cautious one, hesitates. I am finally finding my footing in the city I once called home, establishing a routine, a semblance of normalcy. Would delving into the past unsettle my present?

My gaze shifts from the phone screen to the darkened path ahead. A long, winding road, shrouded in the mystery of the night, just like the path I've been walking since I returned to Bangalore. I take a deep breath, feeling the cool night air fill my lungs. The answer, I realize, lies not in ignoring the message, but in confronting it, in understanding what it truly means to me. The future, after all, is not a straight road, but a path that takes unexpected turns. And this message from Aisha, it's nothing but another turn on my journey, one that I need to navigate, no matter how uncertain or daunting it seems.

And with that, I reach for the phone, my heart pounding in my chest. It's time to face the past, and in doing so, find the direction for my future.

14th February 2014

As I lay my eyes upon Aisha's message, my heart leaps within my chest. "Can we meet?" it asks. A rush of emotions engulfs me, a dance of surprise, eager anticipation, and a hint of apprehension, all draped in a cloak of surrealism.

There's a part of me, a hopeless romantic that clings onto the smallest shred of hope that this could mean something more, while a more practical, self-preserving side braces for disappointment. Yet, amidst the tumult of feelings, my answer is almost instinctive, immediate - "When and Where?"

At this very moment, time seems to stretch, each second echoing loudly in my ears. My gaze fixates on the sent message, the blue ticks confirming her reading of my reply. My heart seems to be rolling and racing just as fast of my wheels, each thump forcing the question, 'What comes next?' As I await her response, my mind races through countless possibilities, painting vibrant scenarios of our impending encounter.

Amidst this whirlwind of thoughts, a peculiar blend of exhilaration and unease takes root in me. After a long stretch of living life on familiar grounds, I find myself on the brink of uncharted territory. The unknown, as I am learning, is both daunting and thrilling.

My phone buzzes again, pulling me back to the present. It's a text from Aisha, specifying the date, time, and location.

Locking the phone screen, I sit back, the enormity of the situation slowly sinking in. I am about to meet Aisha again, after all these years. The prospect sends a tremor of anticipation through me. There's a sense of trepidation, yes, but the undercurrent of hope is hard to miss. It seems like a beam of light has pierced through the predictable monotony of my life, prompting curiosity and unsettling calmness alike.

As I grapple with these feelings, I brace myself for what's to come.

I step into the cafe, the aroma of freshly brewed coffee mixing with the soft hum of ambient music. It's a cozy establishment tucked away in one of the quieter parts of Bangalore, an ambience that is comfortably soothing. As I make my way towards Aisha, the world around me seems to blur into a collage of color and sound. There she is, sitting in a corner, but not alone.

Beside her is a woman, presumably a colleague given her formal attire and the portfolio of documents she's attentively scanning.

The sight takes me aback momentarily. I hadn't anticipated another presence. The knowledge that this meeting was strictly professional sinks in, snuffing out the faint spark of hope that had been kindling within me. Pushing down the twinge of disappointment, I gather my thoughts and walk towards them.

Our initial conversation is mostly formalities and introductions, the atmosphere holding a professional charge. The woman, introduced as Regina, is indeed a colleague of Aisha's, working in her team on a new project they are pioneering. As the meeting unfolds, the realization hits me. This meeting, orchestrated under the guise of a potential business opportunity, had another layer to it.

As Aisha discusses the proposal, I find myself mulling over the newfound context of this meeting. I feel an odd mixture of resentment and gratitude towards my parents for having arranged this. They had been worried about my apparent dissatisfaction with my professional life, and this was their solution.

I give the proposal a cursory read, but my thoughts keep wandering back to Aisha. The Aisha sitting across me, talking numbers and strategies, feels like a completely different person from the one I've been holding on to in my memories. Her confidence and ambition shine brightly, painting a picture of a woman who has clearly carved out a successful path for herself.

As meeting nears its end, we find ourselves caught in an uncomfortable silence. The anticipation, the conversations, the revelations - they converge into a whirlpool of emotions, leaving me slightly disoriented. I observe her gracefully gathering her belongings, her movements imbued with a newfound determination, a resolve I had not witnessed before.

We part ways with a promise to consider the proposal and a polite nod, the absence of our once effortless camaraderie hanging heavy in the air. As I watch her walk away, the Aisha I knew merging with the woman she has become, I feel a pang of...what? Disappointment? Longing? I'm not sure.

I feel a sense of loss, one that's stronger than I had ever experienced. It wasn't just about losing her, it was about losing the image of her I had cherished and held onto all these years. The harsh light of reality casts long shadows on my dreams, leaving me questioning if they were ever viable in the first place.

It feels like I'm standing at the shore, observing the ebb and flow of emotions engulfing me. Every wave and revelation reshapes my perception, illuminating the intricate depths of my inner self. With each surge, the pillars of my past erode, compelling me to reevaluate my reality. It's a bitter pill to swallow, a poignant scene to witness.

I sit there, staring blankly at the now, cold chai in front of me. My heart, however, burns with a thousand questions. Should I confront Aisha about my feelings? Does she deserve to know the turmoil that I've been going through? Or should I spare her the emotional burden?

Each question brings with it a fresh wave of confusion, dousing the feeble sparks of resolution. The internal conflict is intense, threatening to consume me. A part of me longs to confess, to let her know how I feel, how I've always felt. Another part cautions me against it, fearing the consequences, the potential fallout.

As the city's chaos rushes back in with the opening and closing of the cafe door, what should I do? I collect my thoughts, my feelings, and all my years of longing, and stuff them deep into the corner of my heart.

This meeting wasn't just a business proposal, it was a mirror reflecting back the realities I had been avoiding.

The woman I had been longing for had moved on, or so I think, just as I should. But the question is, can I?

23rd April 2014

I find myself locked in the silence of my office, the business proposal laid out before me. The buzz of the fluorescent lights is the only sound cutting through the stillness. The walls of my cubicle feel closer than ever, as though closing in on me. The document stares back at me, its words and figures weaving a tale of future prospects and returns, yet it all feels hollow, much like the silence around me.

I recline in my chair, my gaze lingering on the cream-coloured ceiling tiles. My mind is far from this room though. It's with Aisha. The memory of her from our last meeting flickers to life - her confidence, her fiery spirit, her tenacity. She's better than this proposal, I think. She's made for bigger things, for ventures that challenge her, that ignites her passion, not something that's just enough. An odd sense of protectiveness swells within me, a desire to see her soaring higher, unburdened by the mediocrity this proposal represents.

My mind shifts gears, steering towards the reality of my own professional life. The practice that once felt like my sanctuary now resembles a well-worn path leading to nowhere. Days have blended into weeks, and weeks into months, each passing moment taking with it a bit of the fulfilment I once found in my work. The thought of quitting has been gnawing at the edges of my mind, a frightening yet oddly relieving prospect.

My eyes flicker back to the document, now seeing it as a stark reminder of my discontent. I can't help but draw parallels between this proposal and the stagnancy I feel in my own career. It's a grim reminder of the dissatisfaction I've been wrestling with, leaving a sour taste in my mouth. I'm standing at a crossroads, caught between the comfort of the familiar and the thrill of the unknown.

I must see Aisha. I must tell her my decision, a decision to decline the business proposal, or at least that's the facade I decide to put up. The truth, I confess to myself, lies deeper. It's not about the business proposal, but about her. The irresistible pull towards her, the desire to see her again, is what drives me.

As I begin drafting the message to Aisha, my fingers hover over the touchscreen, uncertain. The three words 'Can we meet?' stare back at me from the screen, a mirror to my anticipation and apprehension. The apprehension of her possible refusal, and the anticipation of meeting her once again.

Swallowing down a knot of unease, I hit send, allowing the ripples of my decision to spread out into the world. As the phone pings back with her swift reply, a meeting date and time agreed upon, I can't help but smile. It seems destiny has granted me another opportunity, a chance to peel back the layers of unsaid words and hidden feelings.

Sitting there in the silence of my office, the enormity of what I'm about to do seizes me. This could be the last time I meet her, the last chance to voice the storm of emotions swirling within me. The thought sends an uneasy shiver through me, but it's one I'm willing to brave.

In the quiet hum of the city night, I find myself grappling with the possibilities. Will this meeting finally provide the closure I've been seeking or open a new chapter in our lives? Can Aisha possibly feel the same way about me, or am I merely clinging onto the remnants of my past?

I find myself at the same cafe, awaiting her arrival. The familiarity of the surroundings only heightens the difference of this encounter, a stark reminder of how much our lives have shifted.

As she steps into the cafe, time seems to slow down, the world fading into a blur around her. Her presence engulfs me, pulling me back into a sea of memories, emotions, and long-lost hopes. The sight of her, the real, tangible Aisha in front of me, sends a pang of longing through my heart. It's her I've been waiting for, not the business proposal or its implications.

We engage in polite small talk, carefully treading around the elephant in the room. As the meeting stretches on, the conversation veers away from the business proposal and becomes more personal. The air between us feels charged with unsaid words, and I can't help but extend the conversation, holding on to every moment I get to spend with her.

Aisha, being the observant woman she is, seems to understand my predicament. A knowing smile dances on her lips as she meets my gaze. "Is there something you'd like to tell me, Rudra?" she asks, her voice carrying a hint of teasing curiosity.

Her question catches me off guard. It's as if she has seen through my charade, peering into the depths of my turmoil. My mind races, searching for the right words. Should I tell her? Or should I hold my tongue? The weight of this moment seems to hang heavily on my shoulders, the silence between us echoing louder than any words I could utter.

Her question, so direct and unexpected, feels like an open door, a chance to finally let my feelings be known. My heart pounds in my chest, a loud, rhythmic drum calling for me to seize the moment. "Yes, Aisha," I manage to utter, my voice barely above a whisper. "There is something I need to tell you."

I swallow hard, the words I've been holding onto for so long finally on the verge of being set free. This is it, the moment of truth, the crux of our relationship. All the unsaid words, the repressed feelings, the lingering hopes, everything converges at this very moment. The course of my life could change with this confession, and I find myself teetering on the edge of a precipice, ready to take the plunge.

This, I realize, isn't merely about the business proposal. It's about me, about Aisha, about the paths we've walked and the roads we're yet to explore. It's about stepping away from what's expected and moving towards what truly resonates with us. And maybe, it's about time I made a choice.

30th October 2021

A few days have turned into weeks, weeks into months and now months into years. Time, that relentless juggernaut, marches on. I find myself ensnared in the web of my work, numbers and graphs, projects and deadlines filling my days with a mechanical rhythm. The pulse of the city, the buzz of the office, and the hum of life around me form a symphony I dance to, yet within the cacophony, a melody lingers—a melody that takes me back to a time of innocence, of joy, of Aisha.

A quiet moment at my desk, a fleeting glance at a passing stranger, or even the particular way sunlight filters through my office window can bring her back to the forefront of my mind. I'll see her eyes, her smile, the way she'd toss her hair back and laugh with abandon. It's a memory, yet it feels as real as the papers scattered before me.

I remember our first dance. We were children then, wide-eyed and unburdened by the world's weight. Her hand in mine felt like the most natural thing, a connection that transcended mere friendship. Our feet moved to the music, but it was our hearts that danced that day—a dance that never truly ended.

But reality has its pull. The dance has become a distant echo, a cherished memory tucked away in the recesses of my mind. Work requires my attention, my dedication, my energy. My career has become the stage on which I now perform, a dance of a different kind. Yet, as I pore over the spreadsheets, analyze the data, and push towards the next big success, the image of that young girl, radiant in her simple dress, haunts my thoughts.

Aisha is there, at the back of my mind, a shadow that follows me, a song that plays in hushed tones. My heart reaches for her, grasps at the essence of what we once were, what we could be. But I push it down, stifle it with reason, and encase it in a practicality that befits a man of my position.

And so, the days turn into nights, and the nights into mornings, in an endless loop. The dance of my youth becomes a metaphor, a symbol of an unspoken yearning. A yearning that's more profound than mere nostalgia, something that tugs at my very soul.

I find solace in my work, a kind of peace in the routine. The numbers make sense, the logic is clear, and the path is laid out before me. But in the quiet moments, when the world falls asleep, and I'm left alone with my thoughts, I hear the music again.

A song that whispers of a time when everything was simple, everything was pure, everything was Aisha.

And I wonder, as I drift into another restless night if she hears it too.

The sun is sinking low, casting golden hues across the city skyline as I make my way home. The weight of the day rests on my shoulders, the hustle of work leaving me both drained and reflective. My mind drifts back to Aisha, like a ship forever anchored to its harbor.

My sister and I have always shared a close bond, and tonight, I feel a sudden urge to talk to her, to confide in her. Dinner is a casual affair, our conversation weaving through the mundane details of our daily lives until I feel the pull to dive into deeper waters.

"You remember Aisha, right?" I begin, my voice trailing off, uncertainty creeping in.

My sister's eyes light up with recognition, and she smiles knowingly. "Of course, Rudra. How could I forget?"

The memories flood back, vivid and vibrant, taking me to the cusp of a new era, New Year's Eve 2000, the Y2K, the break of the millennium. The excitement of the new century was in the air, a promise of new beginnings and endless possibilities. Families and friends had gathered to celebrate, the air filled with laughter, music, and the clinking of glasses.

I was just a young boy then, my parents' gentle nudging urging me to step forward and ask someone to dance. The dance floor was alive with movement and color, but my eyes were drawn to one figure, one person who stood out from the rest: Aisha.

Her presence seemed to light up the room, her laughter contagious, her spirit carefree. I felt a pull towards her, something I couldn't quite understand, a connection that went beyond mere friendship. It was as if we were meant to dance together, a dance that transcended time and space.

With a mixture of nervousness and excitement, I approached her, my heart pounding in my chest. Her eyes widened in surprise as I extended my hand, and she looked at me, her expression a blend of confusion and curiosity.

"Kya line maar raha hai tu?" she asked, her words playful yet probing

Her question caught me off guard, but her teasing smile told me she wasn't really offended. I stumbled over my words, trying to find the right way to express what I was feeling. It wasn't about impressing her or winning her over; it was about sharing a moment, a connection that I felt deep in my soul.

"I just want to dance with you," I finally managed to say, my voice barely above a whisper.

She looked at me, her eyes searching mine, as if trying to decipher the sincerity in my words. And then, as if sensing the truth in my plea, she smiled and took my hand.

The dance that followed was magical, a fusion of youthful innocence and a connection that seemed to transcend our years. We moved together, our bodies finding a rhythm that was uniquely ours, our laughter mingling with the music.

As the clock struck midnight, heralding the new millennium, I looked into her eyes, and I knew. I knew that this dance was just the beginning, a prelude to a relationship that would weave its way through our lives.

The memory is as clear today as it was then, a moment frozen in time, a dance that continues to resonate within me. It was a dance of friendship, of understanding, of connection. A dance that started with a playful challenge and ended with a bond that has lasted through the years.

I realize that the dance has never truly ended. It has evolved, grown, and deepened, but it has never stopped. The connection I felt with Aisha on that New Year's Eve continues to be a guiding force in my life, a connection that I now understand is love.

My sister listens, her expression thoughtful and understanding. When I pause, lost in the whirlpool of emotions, she reaches across the table, her hand resting on mine. "Rudra," she says softly, her eyes filled with empathy, "Maybe it's time you talk to her about how you feel. I've always sensed something special between you two, a connection that goes beyond friendship."

Her words resonate with a truth I've been reluctant to acknowledge. My heart leaps at the prospect, yet fear holds me back. What if I'm mistaken? What if she doesn't feel the same way? What if we lose what we have?

"You'll never know if you don't try," my sister urges, her voice gentle but firm. "Life's too short to keep wondering 'what if.' Maybe she's the answer to the questions you've been asking yourself."

Her words linger in the air, a challenge and a beacon guiding me towards a path I've been too afraid to tread.

The evening wears on, the two of us lost in conversation, laughter, and shared memories. But her words stay with me, etched in my mind, calling me to action.

As I plop onto my bed later that night, the world quiet and still, my phone pings, jolting me from my thoughts. It's Aisha. My heart skips a beat as I read her message. She's got a new job, a fresh start, and she wants to interview me with regards to work.

A smile spreads across my face, a mixture of pride, excitement, and anticipation. This time, I'm sure. This time, I'll tell her. The melody of our dance has never ceased, and perhaps it's time to step back onto the dance floor and move to the music that only we can hear.

I refuse to let fear restrain me any longer. Instead, I will wholeheartedly embrace the dance of life, following it wherever it may lead. And this time, I will fearlessly express my authentic self, speaking my truth with unwavering conviction.

6th November 2021

The day of the interview approaches swiftly, each tick of the clock echoing the beat of my heart. The professional facade, the reason for our meeting, is just a veil thinly veiling my true intention. This meeting with Aisha is not about work; it's about us, about the unspoken words that have lingered between us for far too long.

I stand before my wardrobe, pondering my outfit, a task previously dismissed. It's not merely about impressing her professionally, but conveying something intimately profound. Eventually, I choose a refined and effortless ensemble, an embodiment of my authentic self, with a touch of refinement. As I view the text I sent her via LinkedIn, I sense that it has set everything in motion, as if it holds the power to alter the course of destiny.

The drive to her new office is filled with mixed emotions. My hands grip the steering wheel a little tighter as I navigate through the city streets, my mind racing with what I'm about to say. The words have been forming and reforming in my head, never quite settling into a coherent speech. What if I stumble? What if I falter? What if she doesn't feel the same way?

I shake the doubts away, focusing on the road ahead. The connection we've always shared, the understanding, the bond - it has to mean something. I have to believe that it does.

As I park my car and make my way to her office building, my steps falter for a moment. The building looms large, a symbol of her growth, her success, and her journey. A pang of pride swells within me, mixed with a nervous anticipation.

I'm ushered into a waiting area, a sleek, modern space filled with the quiet hum of business. I glance at the clock on the wall, time moving both too quickly and too slowly. My palms feel clammy, my breath a little shallow. I try to focus on the professionalism of the meeting, but my thoughts keep drifting back to what I really want to say.

When Aisha finally walks into the room, all thoughts of work vanish.

The interview itself is a blur, our conversation weaving effortlessly through work-related topics. Her questions are sharp, insightful, and her interest in my opinions is genuine. Yet, beneath the surface, I can feel something else, a current of unspoken understanding, a dance we're both participating in even as we talk business.

As the official part of our meeting winds down, I find myself at that critical juncture, the moment I've been waiting for. My heart pounds in my chest, a drumbeat of anticipation, fear, and hope.

She looks at me, her eyes searching, as if sensing that there's more to this meeting than just business. The room is quiet, the world momentarily holding its breath.

This is it. The dance floor is open again, the music is playing, and it's time for me to take the lead. I clear my throat, my voice suddenly feeling inadequate for the gravity of what I'm about to say.

"Aisha," I begin, my voice tinged with emotion. "Do you remember New Year's Eve 2000? The Y2K, the break of the millennium?"

She looks at me, her eyes widening slightly, curiosity mingled with understanding. She nods, encouraging me to continue, a soft smile playing on her lips.

I feel the memories flooding back, the excitement of the new century, the nervous anticipation as I approached her on the dance floor. "I remember my mother and father urging me to step forward and ask someone to dance, and all I could see and think of was you," I confess, my voice cracking with emotion. "You were surprised, confused, and you asked me, 'Kya line maar raha hai tu?'"

She laughs at the memory, the sound like music to my ears. "I remember," she says, her voice soft, her eyes sparkling with recollection.

I continue, telling her about our dance, about the connection I've always felt, about my feelings for her. I tell her how that moment has stayed with me, how it was a turning point in our relationship, a dance that has never truly ended.

The room seems to fade away as I lay my heart bare, my voice steady despite the tremor in my hands. The memory of our dance, the rhythm of our connection, resonates in my words.

She listens, her expression unreadable, her eyes fixed on mine. The silence that follows my confession is deafening, the seconds stretching into eternity.

And then, she smiles.

Her smile, genuine and warm, reaches her eyes, and I know, before she even says a word, that the dance is far from over. It's a new beginning, a fresh start, a continuation of the dance we began all those years ago.

"There's something else I wanted to talk to you about, something personal," I say, my voice barely above a whisper.

She leans forward, her eyes inviting me to continue.

"I've always felt this connection with you, Aisha," I confess, my heart laid bare. "It's more than friendship, more than admiration. It's love."

The words I've rehearsed fall away, and I speak from the heart, raw and honest.

6th November 2021 - Aisha

As I sit in the softly lit room, my thoughts drift to the conversation I had earlier with my friend Priya. She had winked at me and said, "Rudra's quite a catch, you know. Smart, successful, and not bad to look at either. Maybe you should make a move."

I'd felt my cheeks warm at her suggestion, but I'd quickly brushed it off. "Come on, Priya, we're family friends. It wouldn't be appropriate."

And yet, as I'd said those words, my mind had flitted back to that New Year's Eve in 2000. I could still feel the warmth of young Rudra's hands as he'd pulled me onto the dance floor, the audacity! I'd been furious at first but also, if I was honest with myself, a little flustered. Who was this boy who'd had the courage to simply walk up and claim a dance with me?

Now, years later, here he was, sitting across from me in a formal setting, no longer the audacious boy but a grown man, and handsome at that. I notice his hands trembling slightly, and I suddenly understand why. My heart races; could it be?

Rudra clears his throat, and for a second, I see a flicker of that young boy in his eyes. "Aisha, there's something else I wanted to talk to you about, something personal."

The room's atmosphere shifts, and I find myself holding my breath. He begins speaking of that long-ago dance, the night neither of us ever spoke about but clearly never forgot. He tells me it was a pivotal moment for him, the night when his feelings for me began to shift into something more. My heart soars and sinks at the same time. This is a point of no return.

He takes a deep breath, looking directly into my eyes. "I love you, Aisha. I have for a long time. I just needed to tell you, to let you know how I feel."

For what feels like an eternity, we're suspended in a silence that's thick with years of unspoken feelings and missed opportunities.

It's as if a door has swung open between us, flooding the room with light and endless possibilities. A future that had always felt just out of reach now seems tantalizingly close, almost touchable. And as we rise to leave the room, our hands still entwined, I realize that our dance has never really ended; it has only just begun.

So, what do I do now? I find myself at a crossroads, no longer teetering on the edge of uncertainty. As the sun sets on this day, my heart is full. I'm filled with a sense of optimism, knowing that whatever comes next, I will be ready to face it head-on.

As I sit across from Rudra, my heart races in anticipation. So much has led us to this moment, and I find myself in awe of the serendipity that has brought us here, on the cusp of a conversation that might just define us. Rudra looks equally nervous and expectant, his fingers drumming lightly on the table.

He reaches for the menu, but I see right through the guise. We're both stalling, avoiding the inevitable conversation that looms before us. It's funny how sometimes, amid the deepest silences, the air becomes thick with words unsaid, emotions unexpressed.

"I think we should skip the formalities," I say, mustering up the courage to slice through the tension. "We both know why we're here."

Rudra looks at me, and for a second, the walls he's built come crumbling down. I see it all—the vulnerability, the yearning, the hope—in the depths of his eyes.

"You're right," he sighs, putting the menu aside and taking a deep breath. "Let's talk."

Rudra's eyes are fixed on me as he says, "I've wanted to have this talk for years, Aisha. I just never knew how, never knew if it was the right time. And honestly, I didn't know if you felt the same way."

The vulnerability in his voice strikes a chord deep within me. I take a deep breath, readying myself to dive into emotional depths we've never explored before.

"Do you believe in the Red Thread Theory?" I ask him, my voice tinged with a kind of hopeful curiosity.

He seems momentarily taken aback by the question. "The Red Thread Theory?"

"Yes," I say softly, locking eyes with him. "It's an ancient belief that a red thread connects two people who are destined to be together, regardless of time, place, or circumstances. The thread may stretch or tangle, but it will never break."

I pause, gauging his reaction. Rudra is silent, but his eyes are alive, curious. I continue.

"I've always felt that there was a red thread connecting us, Rudra. A thread woven through the fabric of our lives, tangling, stretching, but never, ever breaking. Even when we lost touch, even when we were occupied with our own worlds, that thread remained. It's what brought us to that dance floor when we were children; it's what brought us together for that work interview; and it's what brings us here tonight."

My heart is pounding in my chest, the weight of my confession hanging heavy in the air between us. But there's also a newfound lightness, as if I've released a burden I didn't even know I was carrying.

Rudra's eyes search mine as if he's sifting through the layers of my soul, and then he finally speaks.

"I've felt it too," he says quietly, his voice charged with emotion. "Even when I tried to push it aside, focus on work, or convince myself it was just a fleeting thing, I couldn't. You were always there, at the back of my mind, like a song I couldn't forget."

The air between us is electric, buzzing with years of unspoken feelings, misunderstandings, and what-ifs. But here, in this secluded corner of the café, it feels as if those threads are pulling tighter, drawing us closer to the moment we've been waiting for, consciously or not.

So there it is. The red thread isn't just a figment of my imagination; it's not a story I've told myself to romanticize the past. It's real, and it has pulled us to this exact moment, to this conversation, to this incredible brink of possibility.

"We've acknowledged the thread, the connection," Rudra starts, his voice shaking slightly. "So what do we do now?"

I look at him, my eyes meeting his. "The theory also says that if two people are meant to be together, they will find a way to make it happen, no matter the odds."

"So, you believe that?" he asks, almost as if he's afraid to hear the answer.

"With all my heart," I respond. I've never been more certain of anything. "But belief alone isn't enough. We have to commit to finding our way, however twisted or complicated that path might be."

A sense of understanding washes over Rudra's face, as if something once obscured is now vividly clear. "Are you saying—»

"Yes," I interrupt, knowing what he's about to ask. "I'm saying let's give us a real chance. Let's untangle this red thread that binds us, and see where it leads. Let's find our way."

Rudra smiles, his eyes shimmering with unshed tears of joy, relief, or maybe a mixture of both. "I've waited a long time to hear you say that, Aisha."

"Me too, Rudra. Me too," I admit, feeling a tear escape my eye.

For years, that red thread had been stretching, testing the limits of our connection. Tonight, it feels as if we've finally grasped both ends, pulling them tightly towards one another.

7th November 2021

As I close the door behind me, stepping into the familiar confines of my home, a rush of emotions engulfs me. Elation mingles with apprehension, forming a complex tapestry of feelings that I can't immediately unpack. The room seems to close in for a moment as I take a deep breath, steadying myself.

Tonight was more than just another; it was a confession, a pact, a turn in the winding road that Aisha and I have been navigating for years. My heart still pounds at the memory of her words, the idea of the red thread that has bound us through time and circumstance.

I shake my head, as if the physical motion could untangle the knot of thoughts in my mind. I need to process this, to understand what it means—not just for me but for us.

"You're late," my sister remarks as I walk into the living room. She's perceptive, always has been, and I can see the glint of curiosity in her eyes.

"How did it go?" she asks, not wasting time with pleasantries. She'd been the one who encouraged me to take this step, to put my feelings into words, to take the risk. It's as if she's been holding her breath, waiting for this moment as much as I have.

I hesitate, searching for the right words. Should I let her in on the emotional gravity of the evening? Or should I play it cool, given that the path Aisha and I are about to tread is new and delicate?

"It went well," I finally say, my voice laced with a careful optimism. "Really well, actually. We're... we're going to give it a try, see where this goes."

My sister's eyes light up, and for a moment, I see relief wash over her face. But she senses there's more, something I'm holding back.

"You look like you're a million miles away," she observes, her voice tinged with concern. "Is everything okay?"

"Yes," I say, more to convince myself than her. "It's just that... it's complicated. But it's a good kind of complicated."

As I say the words, I realize just how true they are. The emotions, the history, the red thread—all of it is complex. But for the first time, it's a complexity I'm willing, even eager, to embrace.

I catch my sister's eye and offer a reassuring smile. "It's a new chapter," I say softly, almost to myself. "And I can't wait to see how it unfolds."

As my sister leaves me to my thoughts, retreating to her room with a knowing smile, I sink into the couch, my mind whirring like a machine. Her question lingers in the air, mingling with the leftover scent of dinner: "Is everything okay?"

In my heart of hearts, I know it is, but I also know that tonight has opened a Pandora's box of sorts. I think about all the challenges Aisha and I will undoubtedly face—the intricate dance of merging our independent lives, the awkwardness of shifting from friends to something more, the ripple effects this will have on both our families, who've been entwined for years.

And yet, even as I ponder these complexities, there's a profound simplicity that underpins it all, a clarity that cuts through the noise. It's that red thread Aisha spoke about, the unbreakable bond that seems to draw us back, time and time again, into each other's orbits.

But it hasn't been all roses and sunshine. There were times when that red thread felt like a noose, tightening around my neck, binding me to a fate I wasn't sure I wanted.

Your mind is a labyrinth, constantly flashing unwanted memories even when you're trying to be happy.

And there's something about labyrinths: they're designed to confuse, deceive, and isolate. Flashbacks of the trials I faced in America began to resurface. The multicultural melting pot I once imagined turned into a crucible where the fire burned too hot, scalding and distorting me from Rudra, the intellectual explorer, into "that foreign guy."

I felt increasingly like an outcast, my ideas ignored or patronized, my accent ridiculed, my dreams trivialized. My work, my passion, my essence were met not with the comradeship I'd hoped for but instead with veiled disdain, sometimes even blatant racism. The very citadel of knowledge I had revered became my emotional gulag. My every move felt scrutinized, my contributions diminished, my identity questioned.

These were all moments when I wanted to cut that red thread, thinking it would free me, but it never did. The thread stretched, it strained, but it didn't break. And in the end, it pulled me back, right to where I needed to be—by her side, bound by a force greater than us, a force that I'm just beginning to understand.

The emotional rollercoaster of the past years seems both a test and testament to this inexplicable connection. A test we've both navigated, knowingly or unknowingly, and a testament to something profound and, perhaps, predestined.

I smile to myself, feeling a newfound sense of peace settle over me. There are still many unknowns, many intricacies to unravel, but for the first time, I'm not daunted. Instead, I'm excited, eager to explore each twist and turn that lies ahead, comforted by the knowledge that no matter how tangled the path, that red thread will always lead me back to her.

5th February 2023

When the phone rang, and I heard Aisha's mom extend the formal dinner invitation to my parents, it felt like a ritualistic passage—a spoken commitment that we were treading the path towards something far more significant than a mere meal. "We would be honoured to have you and your family join us for dinner this coming weekend," she said. Those words hung in the air long after the call ended, filling the room with a blend of anticipation and gravity.

In the days that followed, my mind was a frenzied playground of thoughts and daydreams. Even at work, where my projects usually offered an escape, I found my focus constantly slipping. The algorithms and data sets in front of me blurred into thoughts of Aisha and our future together. It wasn't anxiety—more like a mixture of keenness and the realization that a pivotal life chapter was about to unfold.

In the stolen moments of calm amid work, my imagination would take over, painting vivid pictures of a future with Aisha. I would catch myself smiling at the thought, only for it to be replaced by a newfound sense of duty and earnestness. This dinner wasn't just about impressing her parents; it was about honoring the years, the emotional layers, and the red thread that had woven its way through both our lives.

To distract myself, I tried to drown in work, challenging myself with complex problems, hoping they'd consume me. But even the knottiest of intellectual challenges couldn't hold my thoughts captive. Aisha seeped into every quiet moment, filling them with both sweetness and an acute sense of responsibility.

I wanted to be prepared, to prove to both our families that the years of friendship had laid a strong foundation for what was to come. Aisha was doing her own preparations, I knew. She was likely turning to her close-knit circle of friends and even the infinite wisdom of the internet. We were both bracing ourselves, getting ready to navigate the time-tested customs that lay before us.

With the dinner date drawing nearer, Aisha and I realize that there's still one important task left to accomplish—finding the perfect shirt for me to wear. In our culture, appearances matter, especially in traditional settings like this one. We both agree that this is an opportunity to make a lasting impression.

Aisha and I walk hand-in-hand into the boutique clothing store, I feel a jolt of excitement run through me. Today's quest isn't just any shopping trip; we're preparing for an event that could mark the beginning of the rest of our lives together. My grip on her hand tightens just a bit, silently assuring her that I'm as committed to this as she is.

"So, what type of shirt are we looking for?" I ask, slightly overwhelmed by the diverse array of fabrics, cuts, and styles before us.

She chuckles, and her eyes twinkle in a way that immediately sets me at ease. "I think a classic, button-down shirt would be good. Maybe something in a light color? It will show my parents that you're thoughtful and have good taste."

I nod, liking her idea and the vision she has for this day. "And what about you? What will you be wearing?"

She paints a picture of her chosen dress in words, a balance of elegance and uniqueness. A rush of affection washes over me. We're both navigating the thin line between our families' expectations and our own individuality, and it's heartening to know we're facing it as a team.

The sales associate, clearly sensing our mission, starts pulling out options. Soon, I find myself in the fitting room with an armful of shirts, each one sending a ripple of anxiety through me. What if none of them are right? But then I try on a light blue, slim-fit shirt with a subtle pattern. The fabric feels soft against my skin, and for the first time today, something feels perfectly right.

I step out to show Aisha, and the look on her face dissolves every ounce of anxiety I've felt. "You look great," she says, her voice tinged with genuine admiration.

Encouraged, I strike a playful pose, trying to model the shirt as best as I can. She bursts into laughter. "Don't quit your day job," she jokes, and our shared laughter dispels the last remnants of tension from the air.

After making the purchase, we share a quiet, knowing glance. This is more than just a shirt; it's symbolic of the life we're building together, one step at a time.

As we drive home, her hand in mine, I reflect on what we've just experienced. I'm gripped by a quiet realization that this is just the beginning. The shirt, her dress, the upcoming dinner—they're all part of a larger, unfolding narrative. But for the first time in a long while, I'm not afraid of what the next chapter holds.

As I pull the car into the driveway and turn off the ignition, the weight of the upcoming dinner and what it symbolizes starts to sink in. Yet, in that weight, there's also a lightness—a sense of liberation that comes from knowing that we're in this together.

I look at Aisha, her profile illuminated by the soft glow of the porch light. The serenity in her eyes reflects my own inner peace, and I feel grateful for this woman beside me, for our shared dreams and the life we're planning.

"So, are we ready for this?" I finally muster the courage to ask the question that has been subtly pressing on both our minds. It's not just a question about a dinner or a shirt, but a larger query about us—our relationship, our families, our future.

Aisha turns her head, her eyes meeting mine with a sense of calm that only she can bring into my life. "As ready as we'll ever be," she says softly. "But what matters is we're doing it together."

Her words echo in the car's confined space, expanding to fill the emotional landscape between us. She's right; the 'together' part is what makes all the difference. That's the constant that has brought us to this moment and the one that will carry us into the future.

Unbuckling our seat belts almost in unison, we step out of the car. I circle around to her side and take her hand, as if to solidify the pact her words have just formed.

We stand ready, not just for a mere dinner or an engagement, but for the intricate maze that is life itself. As the door swings open, we eagerly step into a home that may soon symbolize a fresh start for our two families., I feel my heart swell with a combination of love, hope, and most of all, a profound sense of readiness. We're ready, not because we have all the answers, but because we're willing to find them—together.

7th February 2023

My days settle into a familiar, but hectic routine. Wake up, scan through patient appointments on my phone, grab a quick breakfast, and then rush off to the dental clinic. Filling cavities, root canals, dental cleanings—the schedule is packed, more so because I've taken on a significant role in a community dental health project. This project isn't just about professional growth; it's a chance to make a substantial difference in the community. And with the income and recognition it promises, it also serves as a cornerstone for the future Aisha and I are planning.

By the time the clinic's lights are dimmed and the dental chairs are empty, I find myself exhausted but fulfilled, the last one locking up for the night.

Amid this whirlwind of professional commitments, a soothing ritual has become the highlight of my day. My phone vibrates at exactly 10 p.m., breaking the stillness of my paperwork-laden desk. Aisha's name lights up the screen, and for a moment, the weight of my responsibilities seems to lift.

"Hey," I say as I pick up, my voice instantly softer, warmer.

"Hey, you. How was your day saving smiles?" she chimes in, her voice laced with playful warmth.

I laugh, taking a moment to give her a rundown of the day's surgeries, the challenges of the community project, and, more importantly, the little victories that keep me going. She's all ears, throwing in a question here and a joke there, never failing to amaze me with her ability to gauge just how much conversation I need.

"What's the plan for the weekend?" she asks one evening, steering the conversation toward the impending family dinner.

"I've managed to clear my schedule for Saturday. The project activities are intense but they've been planned well, so it should be manageable. I won't let it interfere with our dinner plans," I assure her, mentally preparing to delegate tasks for that day.

"That sounds perfect," she says, and I can hear the smile in her voice. "And remember, Rudra, we're bigger than these individual challenges. They're just steps we have to climb."

7th February 2023

One evening, as I'm talking to Aisha, she drops a bombshell. Her company is offering her a promotion, one that comes with a transfer to Canada. It's a fantastic opportunity for her, one that she'd be crazy to pass up on a professional level. But personally, it puts us in uncharted territory.

"What do you think I should do?" she asks, her voice tinged with both excitement and apprehension.

My heart sinks momentarily, but then I remember our commitment to face hurdles together. "I think it's an incredible opportunity, Aisha. We'll find a way to make it work, even if it means managing a long-distance relationship for a while."Aisha's Canadian Opportunity

One evening, as I'm giving Aisha an update on the project's progress, she drops a bombshell. Her company is offering her a promotion, one that comes with a transfer to Canada. It's a fantastic opportunity for her, one that she'd be crazy to pass up on a professional level. But personally, it puts us in uncharted territory.

"What do you think I should do?" she asks, her voice tinged with both excitement and apprehension.

"I think it's an incredible opportunity, Aisha. We'll find a way to make it work, even if it means managing a long-distance relationship for a while."

The words are out of my mouth before I even have time to fully process the gravity of the situation. As a dentist deeply rooted in my community, both professionally and personally, the thought of Aisha moving countries is daunting. My mind races through the logistics: the time difference, the distance, the absence of her physical presence in my life. But then another thought overpowers all of those concerns—the vision of Aisha reaching new heights in her career, glowing with the same sense of accomplishment that I feel in my work.

"I mean it, Aisha," I continue, making sure she knows this isn't just a knee-jerk reaction. "If this is something you want—and it sounds like an amazing chance for you—then you should take it. We're strong enough to make it through the distance."

I can hear her sigh, a mix of relief and residual worry. "I was hoping you'd say that, but I'm still scared, Rudra. How are we going to manage everything with me being so far away?"

The vulnerability in her voice pulls at my heartstrings, making me wish I could reach through the phone and hold her. "We'll visit each other whenever we can, and there's always video calls, messages. It's not the same as being together physically, but it'll keep us connected.

And remember, this isn't forever; it's just a chapter in our lives."

She's quiet for a moment, and I sense her weighing the possibilities. "Alright," she finally says, her voice filled with a conviction that I've come to admire immensely. "Let's do this. Let's turn this hurdle into a stepping stone."

The weight of our words hangs in the air long after our call ends, turning my thoughts introspective. This is not the smooth path to marriage that either of us had envisioned. It's fraught with challenges, both immediate like my project and monumental like her move to Canada. But in a way, these hurdles have become our litmus test, a way to gauge the strength of our partnership.

As I lay in bed that night, staring at the ceiling but seeing only a swirl of thoughts, one thing becomes crystal clear: We're not just passively letting life happen to us. We're active participants in shaping our destiny, together. And that realization makes the uncertainties and difficulties not just endurable, but valuable chapters in our unfolding story.

11th February 2023

The sun streams through the curtains, but it feels different today, weighted with the promise and apprehension of the evening ahead. I wake up earlier than usual, despite the late-night consultation calls from patients. Aisha and I had agreed to meet at the venue beforehand to make sure everything was perfect. No room for mistakes today—too much is riding on this dinner.

I take extra care as I shave; I can't afford a nick or a cut today. Glancing at the newly bought outfit hanging on the wardrobe door, I find my thoughts drifting to Aisha. I imagine her doing something similar—preparing, pondering, probably pacing a little. The mirror reflects my face, but the eyes staring back are far away, lost in thoughts of the evening to unfold and the decisions that loom in the horizon.

After a quick breakfast, I look at the note that Aisha had left— "Relax, it will be okay." Taking a deep breath, I grab my car keys and head out.

As I pull up to the venue, a quaint but elegant restaurant we both love, I see Aisha's car already parked. My heart does a tiny somersault—she's always a step ahead, another reason why I admire her so much. I step out of the car, fix my coat, and take another deep breath before walking in.

Inside, Aisha looks radiant as she discusses last-minute details with the restaurant manager. When she sees me, her face lights up, momentarily dispelling the knot of tension in my stomach. We share a quick but meaningful hug—a simple touch that speaks volumes, especially today.

"Everything is set," she whispers, as her eyes search mine, perhaps looking for a clue to the emotional turmoil I've been doing my best to hide.

Just as we share a moment of relief, our families begin to arrive. First my parents, then her parents and her younger sister. The air is thick with anticipation and a hint of nervous energy. Handshakes and pleasantries are exchanged, names are repeated, and just like that, the evening we've been preparing for is set in motion.

As everyone starts moving towards their seats, I take one last glance at Aisha. She's already deep in conversation with my mother, and something about that sight calms me. Despite the challenges we face—my exhaustive project, her potential move to Canada—this feels right.

But that still, small voice inside reminds me of the things unsaid, the emotional currents running deep but not yet surfacing. Shoving those thoughts to the back of my mind, I take my seat at the head of the table, ready to host this unforgettable evening.

I can only hope that this dinner, so meticulously planned, can serve as a metaphor for the life Aisha and I are planning to build—full of love and shared values,

Once everyone is seated, menus are distributed and light conversation fills the room. The waiter comes by to take our orders, and as the starters arrive, the table becomes a carousel of shared plates and tasting forks. My father discusses his recent fishing trip, and Aisha's younger sister talks excitedly about her upcoming college semester.

As the main courses are served, I take a bite but realize I'm not really tasting anything. My senses are attuned to the interactions around the table. Is everyone comfortable? Are Aisha and I successfully merging these two worlds that mean so much to us? I sneak a glance at her across the table, and she gives me an encouraging smile. It's a simple gesture, but it helps me focus on the present.

Dessert arrives, and my father clears his throat, standing up with a wine glass in hand. The room falls silent. "I've known Aisha's family for many years, and tonight makes me even more confident that our children are making the right decision," he begins. "Rudra and Aisha, your mom and I couldn't be prouder. You have our blessings, love, and support on this new chapter in your lives."

The table erupts in a chorus of clinking glasses, and I feel touched by my father's words. Aisha's mother stands up next. "It's comforting to know that Aisha is marrying into a family we've trusted and loved for years. Rudra, you're the son we never had. Here's to a future as bright as the past we've shared."

Glasses clink again, but this time my throat feels tight, overwhelmed by the emotional weight of the evening.

As the evening progresses, the moments of connection between our families only deepen. My sister and Aisha's sister, who have already forged a strong friendship, find themselves engrossed in a discussion about gardening. They eagerly exchange tips on new seed varieties and the joy they find in nurturing plants from bud to bloom. Watching them converse with such genuine enthusiasm reassures me that our two families are merging in the most natural way, a seamless confluence of interests and affections.

A break in the conversation gives Aisha's father and me an opportunity to get talking. Tonight, he was excited. His excitement is contagious, and I find myself momentarily distracted from the worries that have been lurking in the back of my mind. The atmosphere around the table is congenial, as warm as the amber lighting that fills the room.

The connection doesn't end there. My sister and Aisha, who have often collaborated on artistic projects in the past, share a lively discussion about a new art exhibit they're both keen to visit. My mother looks at Aisha and says, "When you join our family officially, we're going to make art weekends a tradition." Aisha's eyes light up, and I can see she's as captivated by the idea as my mother is.

As the evening draws to a close, our conversation naturally shifts to the future: possible wedding dates, honeymoon destinations, and potential places to call home. On the surface, the outlook is thrilling, a glimpse of a shared future filled with promise. Yet, beneath my excitement is a persistent undercurrent of anxiety about Aisha's possible move to Canada.

During a lull in the evening, Aisha and I find a moment to step aside. We slip away from the dining area and into a quieter space where the distant clatter of dishes and the laughter from our families act as a soft backdrop to our private conversation.

"You okay?" she asks, her eyes searching mine. There's a perceptible concern, a subtle recognition that something might be off.

"Yeah, of course," I say, my voice maybe a touch too quick, too assured. "Why do you ask?"

"You just seem... I don't know, a bit distracted tonight."

I pause, tempted to open up about the internal tug-of-war I've been experiencing. But looking at her, seeing the hope and subtle worry in her eyes, I find myself assuring her instead. "It's all good, Aisha. Just a lot on my mind with the project and everything. But tonight has been wonderful."

We return to our families, who are now immersed in a discussion about the wedding—a topic that fills the room with an infectious joy, creating a picture-perfect scene that anyone would envy. As the night comes to an end, warm goodbyes are exchanged, punctuated by expressions of how wonderful the evening has been and the collective anticipation of the wedding. Hugs are given, last bites of dessert are savored, and slowly the room empties, leaving behind the echoes of a joyful gathering.

The dinner may have been a resounding success, bringing our families even more tightly together, but it has also served as a poignant reminder for me. Though I've expressed support for Aisha's potential move, an uneasy feeling settles within me as the night winds down. I can't ignore it any longer. The distance between nations can easily be measured, but the distance between two hearts is a far more complex equation.

22nd February 2023

The phone buzzed on the coffee table, breaking my reflective trance. As I pick up the phone and see Aisha's name flash on the screen, a swirl of emotions engulfs me—relief that she's calling, and apprehension about the lingering thoughts that have been haunting me. "Hey, Aisha," I manage to say, injecting as much cheerfulness into my voice as I can muster.

Her voice comes through, clear and comforting. "How are you, Rudra? Still buzzing from the family dinner?"

"Yeah, it was quite an evening, wasn't it?" I reply, struggling to keep my voice steady. "Everyone seemed to enjoy themselves."

She agrees, and for a moment, I think maybe that's all this call will be—just a pleasant recap of a successful night. But then there's a pause, and I can almost feel her collecting her thoughts on the other end.

"Rudra," she finally says, her tone shifting subtly, "I've been thinking. Something felt a bit off during the dinner.

Not with our families—they were great—but with you. Is everything okay?"

My heart starts pounding in my chest. This is the moment. I have the choice to open up about what's really been bothering me or keep it all inside. I hesitate, every second stretching out as if time has decided to slow down just to accentuate my indecision. The pause may have lasted only a moment, but in relationships, a moment can say a thousand words. Words I haven't yet found the courage to speak.

Should I tell her? Should I pour out everything that's been plaguing my thoughts—the fear, the love, the unsettling notion of distance and sacrifice? The weight of my silence grows heavy, and I realize I can't bear it any longer.

Taking a deep breath, one that I hope doesn't betray my emotional tumult, I finally speak. "Aisha, there's something we need to talk about."

And just like that, the walls I had built start to crumble, making way for a conversation that could very well be our turning point.

The tension in the air seems to quiver with potential energy, like a rubber band stretched to its limit. "I've been doing some thinking," Aisha begins. "About us, our future, and the move to Canada."

I brace myself, not sure what to expect. She takes a deep breath and continues. "I've decided to stay back, Rudra. I've turned down the job offer in Canada."

For a split second, time freezes. The words I've secretly longed to hear, but have been afraid of confronting, hang in the still air between us. My first instinct is to celebrate, to shout in joy, but a wave of emotion overwhelms me, complex and multi-layered.

"Really?" is all I manage to say, my voice trembling with an emotional cocktail of relief, love, and an inexplicable touch of guilt.

"Yes," she replies, sensing but not yet fully grasping the depth of my conflict. "I've found another opportunity here, and the more I thought about it, the more it felt right."

I should be elated, ecstatic even. And part of me is, but another part is swimming in guilt. As much as I love her and want her close, I never wanted to be the anchor that holds her back from soaring. The irony of my situation hits me—I'd been struggling with the thought of her leaving, and now I find myself struggling with the idea of her staying for me.

"Aisha, you have no idea how much it means to me that you're staying," I finally say, my voice tinged with emotion. "But I have to ask, are you sure about this? I love you, and the last thing I want is for you to give up your dreams because of me."

She reassures me that it's her choice, that she hasn't abandoned her dreams but merely shifted the path she'll take to achieve them. "This isn't just about compromise, Rudra. It's about building a life together, here, where our roots are."

Her words bring both solace and a newfound understanding of the compromises and decisions that come with love. And as we continue to talk, affirming our commitment to focus on local opportunities and to build our future together, I realize that the true turning point isn't just Aisha's decision to stay. It's the collapse of the emotional walls between us, making room for a future filled with collective dreams, side by side.

As I sit in the silence that follows the end of our call, my heart still pounding from the emotional rollercoaster, I can't help but feel that today marks a new chapter in our story—one penned with the ink of sincerity and openness. For so long, we've both danced around the edges of a significant decision that could have reshaped our lives in profound ways. Now that decision has been made, and not unilaterally, but as a result of a dialogue between two people who are learning what it means to truly be partners.

A wave of relief washes over me once more, but this time it's accompanied by a sense of mature understanding. I'm starting to comprehend the true gravity of what it means to share a life with someone, to make choices not just for oneself but for the sake of a shared future. And this realization doesn't scare me as much as I thought it would; instead, it fills me with a newfound respect for the woman I love—for her ability to make hard decisions, to communicate openly, and to consider us a team.

In a way, this call, this decision, these complex feelings—they're all tokens of a relationship that's ready to evolve. No longer are we just a young couple in love, but two adults committed to navigating whatever challenges life throws our way. And I know there will be challenges, more decisions, more turning points. But for the first time, I feel fully equipped to face them, and I know Aisha does too.

I realize that our love isn't just about the romantic dates, the whispered "I love yous," or the easy laughter that's always come naturally to us. It's also about these hard conversations, the unspoken fears, the sacrifices, and the compromises. It's about navigating through life's messiness and still choosing each other, every single day.

And as I sit there contemplating this new chapter we've just begun, I can't help but feel incredibly grateful—not just for the love that Aisha and I share, but for the life we're about to build, one honest conversation at a time.

29th October 2023

As I open my eyes, a profound sense of calm washes over me. It's not just another day; today, Aisha and I will become a single entity in the eyes of the world. A rush of excitement courses through my veins at the thought, replacing my initial tranquility. I get up, shower, and dress in the traditional attire chosen for this special occasion.

My family and I arrive at the venue with plenty of time to spare. The atmosphere has been transformed into an enchanting garden, illuminated by twinkling fairy lights and adorned with fragrant flowers. It perfectly reflects Aisha's love for all things botanical. As I take in the scene, I notice the unique details that make this day truly our own—the vibrant colors, the exquisite floral arrangements, the melodic music, and the delicate art installations scattered throughout the venue. I can't help but notice the adorable, intimate touches that give life to our personal story. The table settings include small hand-painted stones, a crafty weekend project Aisha and my sister undertook, each stone featuring symbols or words that have special meaning to us. On the other side, a cute little garden station is set up where guests can plant a seed in a pot and take it home with them as a unique wedding favor.

I find myself feeling overwhelmed and deeply moved by the beauty of this day, so much care and effort went into every aspect of our wedding celebration. Each element evokes memories and aligns with Aisha and my personal experiences and preferences.

As the guests start to arrive, their expressions mirror the joy and unity that resides within me. Our families have shared a long-standing friendship, and today, they will blend into one cohesive unit. A profound sense of wholeness envelops me; it feels as though every step I've taken in my life has led me to this remarkable moment.

I stand there, waiting for Aisha, my heart pounding in anticipation. The music shifts, signaling that the moment has arrived. All my doubts and fears about the future dissipate. I realize that as long as we remain together, every challenge becomes conquerable, and every joy becomes more profound.

Today isn't just a celebration of our love; it's a manifestation of the unity and joy that has always existed between our families, now sealed in an eternal bond.

As Aisha steps up beside me, and we begin the cherished rituals that will unite us in matrimony, I feel as though our twin flames are finally merging into one, igniting a love that will burn brightly for a lifetime.

The moment I see Aisha in her wedding attire, my heart swells with emotion. She looks ethereal, bathed in the soft glow of the ceremonial lights. As she steps forward, a vision in flowing fabric and intricate embroidery, I feel as if the universe has paused just for us, preserving this image in the tapestry of my memories.

Amid the rituals, my thoughts naturally return to a concept that has already been a recurring theme in our relationship—the red thread theory and the idea of twin flames. This ancient belief posits that those destined to meet are connected by an invisible red thread, a bond that can stretch or tangle but never break. The theory had captivated us both when we first heard it, and through the ebbs and flows of our relationship, it felt like a prescient tale. Today, as I look at Aisha, I feel the palpable force of that invisible red thread tightening, pulling us even closer in this sacred moment.

We decided to transform this symbolic concept into a tactile reality for our wedding. As the priest chants the final hymns, Aisha and I each hold onto a red thread. With each vow we make, we loop the threads into a knot, each twist symbolizing a commitment, a promise, a unifying bond. "Just as these threads have intertwined, so have our lives," I say, the weight of the moment filling my voice.

Aisha's eyes meet mine, shimmering like a night sky full of promises. It's as if in this moment, our theory of being twin flames—the other halves of the same soul—has been made flesh and thread.

I recall the moment when Aisha accepted my LinkedIn proposal—a modern yet fitting symbol of our union.

The day I gave Aisha a promise ring resurfaces as another cornerstone—a tangible commitment that held the essence of our affection, binding us in the sacred 'prelude' to what we have now.

Then there's the day marked by the exchange of engagement rings. Each glint from the diamonds that day mimicked the sparkle in Aisha's eyes, further solidifying that we were in a deep, mutual commitment to walk this journey of life together.

A special weight is held by the day we put words into actions, the day we signed the 'enlightenment document' during our Gurudwara wedding ceremony. It wasn't just a contract; it was a tangible manifestation of our core beliefs and intentions for our shared life.

Every moment we shared held special significance, intricately connected and leading us to this sacred finale. As I stand here now, I can't escape the feeling that each served as a milestone on the map of our relationship. The scarlet thread we now hold might be a recent addition to our shared history, yet it's woven from the same cherished fabric as those moments that shaped us.

As the ceremony concludes, we take our first steps as a married couple, our fingers entwined much like our red threads. In this magical moment, awash in a sea of love and joy from our families, I feel a profound sense of completeness. It's as if the red thread of fate, always present yet invisible, has finally manifested itself, leading us from serendipitous encounters to this pivotal juncture. With Aisha by my side, I know that we're stepping into a new, thrilling chapter, one penned by destiny but written day-by-day by us.

Epilogue

You know, life is a series of interconnected moments—some filled with joy and beauty, others tinged with hardship and pain. It's a dynamic blend of highs and lows, triumphs and setbacks. We've all experienced these ups and downs, haven't we?

Here's the thing about difficult times: they're not permanent. As much as it sounds like a well-worn cliché, it's a truth that remains constant. I remember going through a period when everything seemed to be falling apart. I was entangled in a web of stress and self-doubt, unable to see even a glimmer of hope on the horizon. Yet, as time moved on, that challenging chapter came to a close, just like the happier chapters that had come before it. One day, I found myself stepping out of that darkness, entering a new phase filled with possibility and joy.

Navigating the highs and lows of life isn't only about recognizing their fleeting nature; it's also about learning from every experience. There's always something to glean, something to be grateful for. When you're in the midst of hardship, pause for a moment, take a deep breath, and remind yourself, "This too shall pass." Because, invariably, it will. Just like the seasons inevitably change, so do the circumstances of your life.

Moreover, don't withhold your gifts from the world, even when you're struggling—be it love, kindness, or a simple act of generosity. What you give has a way of circling back to you, often when you least expect it but most need it. So spread goodness, even when you're not feeling particularly good yourself. Trust that it will come back to you.

Life's rhythm of ups and downs will continue; that's the one thing you can count on. But as long as you maintain hope and keep contributing positively to the world, life will reciprocate in kind. Just as Aisha and I discovered each other amidst the complexities of existence, connected by a red thread of destiny, so too are there bonds waiting for you to find, form, and cherish.

Hope is not merely a fleeting emotion, but a life-sustaining force that carries us through times of uncertainty and despair. Along my journey, moments of ambiguity clouded the path ahead. Yet, it was hope that acted as a bridge, providing me with strength and courage to envision a united life, despite the odds stacked against us. The very hope we nurtured became a guiding light, illuminating the darkest days, reminding us that better times were not mere possibilities, but an inevitable certainty.

And then there's the magic of giving. The universe operates on a principle of reciprocity: what you put out often comes back to you in ways you could never foresee. When Aisha decided to stay back instead of moving to Canada for her dream job, she was giving up something significant for us, for our future together. Little did she know that this act of giving would open doors to other incredible opportunities that neither of us could have imagined. The same goes for smaller acts of kindness. Whether it's listening intently to a friend in need, offering a seat to a stranger, or even being kind to oneself after a failure, these acts of giving have a ripple effect. They enrich the giver, the receiver, and the world at large. The act of giving, whether big or small, has an uncanny way of returning to you, often magnified and in the most unexpected ways.

There are different ways in which people unknowingly control each other. To be aware and enlightened is vital.

Emotions & Religion: It's crucial to understand your emotions. First, accept that you have the emotion. Then, consider the situation it will create if you follow through with the emotion and determine whether it will make you happy in the future. Let the feeling guide you.

Being "Extra Nice or Too Helpful": When someone is not genuine but is extra nice or too helpful, it can be a means of manipulation. People might hope they can have others do their bidding this way. You should always remember you have the ability and right to say 'No.' It's essential to thank them for their help but also to understand that you need none; you are capable of helping yourself.

Money: Some use money to exert influence and authority. Avoid greed. Enjoy the simple things in life, and money will come at the appropriate time, allowing you to enjoy it fully. Give, share, and abundance will follow, for even money enjoys being loved.

Dependency: Some might try to provide for all your needs, keeping you dependent on them. Their aim? To instill a fear that if they leave, you'll be helpless. Always remember that you are capable of independence.

Physically: Whether through force or pleasure, some try to ensnare you into servitude. Chains and pain can be overcome with a strong will, and lust should never become an addiction but remain a way to bond in love.

Happiness: If you put your happiness in the hands of others, you give them the power to take it away. A true free spirit knows that their happiness is internal and untouchable.

Promises & Lies: Some might make promises or lie to get you to do things for them, giving you hope for the future. It's important to remember that the past is an experience, the future a lesson, and only the present truly exists. Actions always speak louder than words.

Invoking Divinity: Beware of those claiming to speak the word of God. Listen within you and trust your feelings.

Making You Feel Good: Through jokes and banter, individuals can make one another feel good. It's essential to discern the intent behind the humor, especially if it might be playing with someone's feelings. Trust your intuition.

Love: Love that exists for one's benefit or keeps another from growing is manipulative. True love lays down no controls; it provides freedom.

So as you turn the pages of your own life story, I encourage you to find your red thread—the bond, the purpose, or the passion that gives your life meaning. It could be a person, like Aisha is for me, or a calling that sets your soul ablaze. It's these red threads that not only connect us to our deepest selves but also to the larger tapestry of human experience.

The small miracles that unfold every day—the smile from a stranger, the call from an old friend, the sunset that paints the sky—are often the universe's way of reminding us that life is beautiful. Cherish them. Love deeply, give generously, and never lose sight of hope, for it's these very elements that make life worth living. Keep your heart open, your spirit resilient, and who knows? Your life might just turn into a series of beautiful chapters, each better than the last.

Love for no reason...

When the heart hurts, The love flows,

For what does the heart know, For the purpose to know,

Is just a feeling to show, Everything has to flow,

Life has its way and we are just a soul, Looking for a compatible soul

One to treasure and love and hold, For lo and behold

What do we know as life unfolds, That everything that is cold

Shall find meaning deep in our soul, So we can cherish that soul

That we decide to hold, Close close in our hold

Forever and more in our hearts we are told, This is a soul mate and love to keep so we are told

So we wait and hold for that moment to unfold, Where the curtains unfold

For fairy tales like these are to be told, To young and old

For life is not just a dream but a reality, To titillate, create and relate,

And so we Thank the stars together, That we are part and parcel of the journey of Life together.

Hoping for more and more, Forever and more...Forever and more...

Hope!

Dedicated to my wife

www.ingramcontent.com/pod-product-compliance
Lightning Source LLC
LaVergne TN
LVHW091117150826
845673LV00002B/876

* 9 7 9 8 8 9 1 3 3 9 2 6 2 *